Jasper Joshua

CW00433006

Children for Sale

Second Hand

Second Hand

Children for Sale

SECOND HAND

Jasper Joshua West

Second Hand

Table of Contents

Jasper Joshua West

Get your FREE eBook!

Get your FREE copy of Escaped! bookHip.com/lkcwpk

Just type in **bookHip.com/lkcwpk**

Prologue

SHERRY GRIPPED JAMIE'S HAND throughout the drive. She had a firm grip, and he could feel her nails digging into his skin. It hurt a bit but he didn't have the heart to break her hold. They needed each other now, more than ever, and he was going to be there for her, in whatever way he could be.

The van traveled through the night, heading through the hills outside of the city, though they could still see the lights in the distance. They appeared to be making lots of turns, as if they were trying to avoid the main roads, instead using less-traveled side roads which had lots of potholes. These roads likely had fewer police patrolling, Jamie thought.

Talking with Sam while the man had been recovering had certainly been instructive on how the criminal element worked in a city like this. A city like Cartagena, Columbia. One that, as an 11-year old American boy, he shouldn't know much about.

They finally started heading back into the city, moving close to the tall buildings that marked the city center. They pulled into an alley behind a tall building on the edge of town, then stopped in front of a large door, which slowly rose to admit the van.

Jamie looked over to Sherry, who still looked a little scared, but they didn't appear to be in any immediate danger, even as they moved down into the underground garage of the building.

The van came to a halt and the men outside were speaking quickly in Spanish, too quickly for Jamie to understand. Jamie and Sherry were dragged from the van with their hands secured behind their backs with plastic cable ties. One of the men opened a steel door with peeling paint, revealing a staircase which they started walking up.

"Where are we?" Sherry asked, looking around as they marched up the interminable flights of stairs. No one answered her.

As they passed the doors leading into the different floors, Jamie caught sight of carpeted hallways, with doors on either side with numbers on them.

"I think we're in some kind of hotel," Jamie replied, and Sherry looked up to him, her bright brown eyes wide. "We're going to be okay. I'm going to be with you."

As they stepped out of the stairwell into a hallway, Jamie realized that Sherry was being held back from following him.

"No!" Jamie growled, pulling out of the man's grip.

The man laughed, reaching down to grab at Jamie's arm again as he tried to get back to the stairs.

"No, Sherry!" Jamie shouted, shrugging the man off, and when he tried to grab again, Jamie turned back, seeing the man with his head lowered.

Jamie jerked his head forward and felt the man's nose connect with his forehead. It made a loud, satisfying crack.

"Puta madre!" the man shouted, clutching at his bleeding nose. Jamie didn't know exactly what this meant, but it was a bad word and had something to do with mother. The other men reached out to grab him.

He tried to kick them away, tried to hit another with his head. When they tried to cover his mouth to stop his screaming, Jamie bit at their fingers.

All he could see were Sherry's wide eyes, watching as he tried to fight them off. They were all adults. They were bigger and stronger than he was, certainly bigger than Sherry, who was a year younger and a fair bit smaller than him. And there were four of them. But he had to try anyway. He wasn't going to let them separate him from Sherry if he could help it.

"Kill this little coño!" one of the men shouted, and Jamie pulled free, trying to reach the door.

More hands grabbed his shoulder, and as Jamie tried to wriggle free of their grip, he felt something prick him in the neck. It felt like a bee sting, almost imperceptible in the state that he was in, but a few seconds, he could feel himself losing control over his limbs.

His vision blurred, and the door closed between him and Sherry.

"No... Sherry..." he tried to say, but it felt like he was talking through a mouthful of cotton.

He was falling back. He could see the ceiling now instead of the closed door. He tried to say something, but nothing came out.

More hands reaching for him. Blackness.

Chapter One

JAMIE KNEW THIS FEELING all too well. The feeling of being drugged

He opened his eyes slowly and let out a soft groan while turning over in his bed. There were a horde of aches and pains all over his body, but the dryness in his mouth and the dull, pounding headache were signs that he had been drugged. He tried to remember where he was or how he had gotten there, but his mind was all mixed up.

He'd felt the same way when he woke up on the submarine after being kidnapped from his school in Massachusetts. Jamie rubbed his temples in an attempt to get rid of the pounding in his head, or at least give it a bit of a rest as he pushed up from his bed.

He had no real memory of having arrived in this place.

As the realization dawned on him, Jamie blinked a few times to adjust his eyes to the darkness around him. He was in a room with a group of bunks, most of which were empty, except for one where he could see a boy about his own age asleep.

With a soft groan, Jamie pushed himself up from the bed, feeling the world spin around him for a few seconds. He maintained a grip on the top bunk above him to keep from falling over, then a sweeping sense of nausea hit him.

"Great," he grumbled under his breath. "First thing I want to do is throw up..."

But nothing came, and the sensation passed in a few seconds. Eventually, the world stopped spinning, and he was able to stand up normally.

His mouth was still dry and tasted like sour milk. The room around him smelled even worse; he picked up some strong body odor and the distinct, sharp smell of cigarette smoke, mixed with a strong, sour smell that he couldn't identify. The combination made him want to throw up again.

He still felt like nothing was going to come up though, and after a few minutes of recovering on his feet, Jamie was finally able to walk around the room. He walked quietly, since he didn't want to wake the sleeping kid. As he moved around, he started to feel a little better, and the memories of the trip here started trickling back. Carlos kicking them out in the middle of the night, the long trip in the van. Sherry.

"Sherry," Jamie said aloud, suddenly feeling his heart race. He forgot all about being quiet. "Sherry!"

He needed to find her. The kidnappers tried to separate them, but Jamie had fought back, for all the good that it had done.

The room and shared bathroom appeared to take up the entire floor, since the only other door he could see led into a stairwell. Memories of living with Carlos came back as he quickly walked down the stairs. It hadn't been great dealing with Carlos's anger almost every day, especially after he'd kicked out Maria, so Jamie had been glad to get out of there. But was this place worse? What was this place?

He moved down the steps, rubbing his sinuses. That was going to annoy him for a while; he knew that from being drugged before.

There was nothing about this place that Jamie liked and the sour smell was following him everywhere he went. It now reminded him of milk that had gone bad.

"Maybe this place was a milk factory or something," he thought to himself, reaching the next floor. The stairs kept going down for at least another five floors, but Jamie wasn't sure what he would find at the bottom. When he reached the bottom there were voices coming from beyond the door. He leaned in closer, narrowing his eyes, trying to figure out what he would find in there.

He would need to talk to someone to find out where Sherry was. He needed to get away with her; maybe together they would find a way to get back home.

Jamie took a deep breath and twisted the handle.

Chapter Two

THE DOOR CREAKED loudly and shuddered against the rusty hinges, making Jamie's entrance as loud and conspicuous as possible. Even so, it didn't seem to attract much attention. There was already a great deal of noise coming from inside the room, and those closest to the door briefly glanced over to see him, but the rest appeared too enthralled in their own business to really care.

It looked like a common room, shared amongst a group of about fifty other children. Most of them were seated on long benches in front of wooden tables, talking and playing cards. There were six adults in the room too, but they were all siting together on the far side. Some of the adults were also playing cards but others just sat smoking, or drinking. A TV was on a table near where the adults were sitting, but no one seemed to be watching as it burbled away in Spanish, not loud enough to be heard over the din of kids talking. The adults seemed to put as little interest in their apparent job of watching over the children as was possible, only glancing briefly up to scan the room then returning to their own conversation.

The kids were mostly girls, and from what he could tell, some appeared to be around his age, some a few years older. The boys were older, about 13 or 14, he thought, looking at their faces which had pimples and bits of facial hair. They were also bigger than Jamie. It was the boys who looked up as Jamie walked through the room, but after a brief glance, they quickly turned back to their games.

Maybe they just thought that Jamie wasn't big enough to pose a threat. As far as he could tell, he was the only American; most of the children had the dark skin, hair and eyes of Latinos.

"Sherry?" Jamie called, barely able to get his raspy voice above the din around him. Jamie was starting to feel a little desperate now. He moved through the crowded tables, trying to find the girl he had promised to protect, no matter what. He wasn't sure if it was a promise that he could keep, but he was going to do his best.

"Have you seen a girl?" Jamie asked one of the smaller groups, but they ignored him. "Her name is Sherry, have you seen her? She's ten, with curly brown hair, freckles on her nose?" He thought for a moment, then added, "She's American," which made a few of the boys laugh. That meant at least some of them understood English but were just ignoring him.

Jamie tried again, this time speaking in his broken Spanish. Finally, one of the adults on the far side of the room saw him and walked over.

The man wasn't tall, but he looked strong. He had a thick black mustache and a hard-looking face. He wore a t-shirt with the sleeves torn off, revealing big muscles and plenty of tattoos. Jamie could see a large knife in a sheath attached to his belt, and when the man placed a hand on Jamie's shoulder, his first instinct was to pull away, but his grip was too firm.

"You come with me," the man growled. He wasn't asking. He pushed Jamie over to and through one of the doors near to where the other men were sitting.

There he found Sherry lying on an old leather couch. He pulled away from the man's grasp and rushed over to her. When he put a hand on her shoulder, she stirred and opened her eyes.

"Jamie?" she asked, blinking slowly, needing a second to see him. "I thought… you fought with the men… are you okay?"

"What did you do with her?" Jamie snapped, looking back at the man still standing at the door.

"She scream, we give her medicine to sleep," the man said, then chuckled "Here, kids have no mama, no papa. New home here, okay?"

Jamie didn't answer. He turned back to Sherry and held her hand in his, feeling the relief washing over him like an overwhelming wave. At least they were together.

"Are you alright?" Jamie asked, wiping sweat beads from her forehead. "Did they hurt you?"

She shook her head slowly. "No, I'm not hurt. I feel sleepy and a little sick, that's all."

"It's the drugs," Jamie said softly. "Just take it slow until they wear off. Are you thirsty?" He looked around for the man who had brought him in, but he was gone. Another man was tapping away at his phone, ignoring him and Sherry.

She nodded, smiling and leaning into his hand. "I'm glad you're okay and we're still together."

"Yeah," Jamie said softly. "So am I. But where are we? What is this place?"

Chapter Three

IT TOOK A FEW HOURS for the drugs to wear off. When the men brought in food, the smell made Jamie's stomach growl. He couldn't remember when he'd eaten last, but his stomach was completely empty now.

It was just rice and beans, but it was hot and filling; Jamie and Sherry found themselves attacking their plates and getting a second helping from the large pot which sat on a table in the middle of the room.

Jamie wasn't going to leave Sherry's side again, he vowed. He was going to do everything that he could to make sure that she was safe. They would have to kill him if they wanted to separate them again. They hadn't known each other long, but what they had been subjected to over the past few months had resulted in them forming a bond that was unbreakable.

Once they were finished eating, the children were quickly directed up the stairs towards the same room full of bunks where Jamie had woken a few hours ago. Most of the children appeared to readily jump to the orders, making Jamie wonder why they weren't fighting back. There weren't as many people here, and Jamie didn't know where the other people had gone, but there were at least thirty kids and only four adults. But everyone followed orders. Maybe they were beaten if they disobeyed, he thought.

Jamie's only responsibility, as he saw it, was to keep Sherry safe. As he had done at Carlos's house, he started thinking about how he could escape, but this time, he needed to take Sherry with him. He didn't know what all the girls were wanted here for, but he got the feeling it wasn't good. No way would he leave Sherry here alone, not even if he was going to get help.

They were separated quickly into groups of boys and girls and then guided into large bathrooms on opposite sides of the room. They boys' room had a line of six showers on a single wall. There was no privacy and no walls, but Jamie was used to that by now from his time at the hideout in the forest. The boys stripped down and put their clothes in piles on a wooden bench, then waited their turn in the showers. Jamie followed suit, joining the end of the line. The six shower heads all ran continuously and as each boy finished and left, he was immediately replaced by the next boy in line. When they finished, the boys each grabbed a tattered towel from a heap on a table, dried off, tossed it in the basket and went back to the bench where they had left their clothes. One man stood looking bored by the table with the towels, holding a piece of wood about the size of a baseball bat but that looked more like a table leg. There wasn't any trouble, but this man appeared to be ready.

Noting the body hair now visible on the other boys, Jamie confirmed his suspicion that he was indeed the youngest, and probably the weakest. Some of these boys might be older than he thought. Would he be able to protect Sherry?

Jamie finished up, left the bathroom and quickly found Sherry in the crowd, and stayed by her side. She seemed happy to see him, and grasped his hand in hers as they chose bunk beds in which to sleep.

Like the showers, the bunk beds were designated for boys and girls, but as Jamie was unwilling to part with Sherry again, they chose two free beds in the middle of the room which formed the dividing line between the two sections.

That didn't go unnoticed by the others. A few moved over to where Jamie and Sherry were setting up, watching them closely.

"What are you looking at?" he snapped, turning to face them.

A few of them, mostly girls, quickly backed away, but those who remained came a little closer.

"I'm Juanito," one of the boys said in English. He had his hair shaved almost down to his scalp, and he looked about thirteen years old. "We're just wondering…"

"She's my sister," Jamie lied.

"Oh," Juanito said, scratching his head. "Well, you don't want to be around her when they take her out for a ride. They maybe take you too, you know? Young gringo boy, maybe rich men think you're cute, no?" The other boys laughed at this and spoke amongst themselves in Spanish.

"Where will they take us to for a ride?" Jamie asked, feeling his stomach sinking a bit as the other boys around Juanito started making rude gestures. The one that seemed pervasive was a forefinger pushing into a circle made by the other hand's thumb and forefinger.

"I won't let them take her," Jamie growled, moving back to the bed.

"If you say so," Juanito said, shrugging. He looked like he didn't believe Jamie.

A guard announced in Spanish it was time for bed. Juanito and the other boys moved back to their bunk beds, then the lights went out. The room was still dimly lit from the lights in the bathrooms and after a few moments Jamie could see in the gloom.

Sherry took the top bunk bed, while Jamie took the bottom. It was now dark outside the windows, it was nighttime, but they had spent most of the day sleeping and they weren't very tired now.

Jamie laid trying to sleep and thinking about their situation. When he heard some noise, he turned to see the group of boys he'd seen with Juanito earlier sneaking into the girls' section. They led a young girl over to one of the unused bunk beds. They were trying to be quiet, but Jamie could tell they were excited.

One of them stopped to look over at Jamie and Sherry. He whispered something to his friends and they looked over to Jamie and Sherry. Then three of them approached, the other three staying with the other girl, who was now taking off her clothes.

Jamie knew somehow, they were coming for Sherry. They wanted to take her away like they had the other girl and make her take her clothes off. They were bigger than Jamie, but he wasn't going to allow that to happen.

Jamie stood up when they got closer, putting himself between the boys and Sherry and crossing his arms, facing them. They all stood taller than him, but he wasn't going to let them past without a fight. They gestured for Jamie to move and said something in Spanish which he didn't understand; they clearly wanted him out of the way.

Jamie didn't move, clenching his fists at his sides as they got closer.

One tried to push him aside, but Jamie stood his ground. The one closest to him tried again, and Jamie pushed back, then threw a fist at the boy's face. It connected, but it caused a shot of pain up his arm.

"Ouch," Jamie grunted as the boy fell back, bleeding from his lip.

The other two boys advanced quickly on Jamie, then the boy who he had struck got up and joined them. Jamie threw a few more punches, but the other boys blocked them. Someone kicked him in the stomach. A huge fist hammered into the side of his head, making the world spin.

He desperately attempted to throw a few more punches, as well as a few kicks but he was soon knocked to the floor. One of the boys pinned his arms. More kicks came, knocking the breath out of his lungs.

"Oye!" one of the adults called, hearing the commotion.

The boys scattered, heading back to their own beds quickly before the lights came on.

"*Que pasa?*" one asked, coming over to find Jamie bruised and battered, nursing his bloody lip. "What happened here?"

Jamie looked up to see Juanito's friends looking at him from their beds.

He knew better than to rat on them.

"I fell," Jamie lied.

Jasper Joshua West

Chapter Four

THE GUARDS DIDN'T BELIEVE him, but they weren't being paid enough to care, apparently. The lights went off again, and they all went to bed. The boys didn't come back, and the girl who had been ushered over to their section of room earlier also went back to their own beds.

Even so, with the pain from the beating, Jamie wasn't able to sleep. Not that he thought he was going to get much anyway.

Eventually, he did manage to doze off for a couple of hours before the lights came back on.

He was tired, but not getting any sleep at night was something that Jamie was getting used to. It wasn't something that he particularly liked, but it was a part of his life that he had been living with for almost two years.

As he quickly made his bed, he noticed that Sherry was still asleep, but he didn't have the heart to wake her. Even so, a couple of the boys approached them.

Jamie straightened up quickly, expecting another fight, but these weren't the same boys who had beat him the night before.

They backed away when they saw him, speaking quickly in Spanish. Or at least, it sounded like Spanish, but he still couldn't understand it.

Finally, one came forward who was a little older than Jamie, with a tougher look to him.

"You don't worry, yes?" he said, his English better than Jamie had heard from their guards. "We are not here to hurt you. Just want to say… good that you stood up to the other boys. They hurt the girls. The guards don't like it, but nobody says who they are, or they hurt you too, right?"

Jamie nodded. He figured that was the case among the children.

"But if you learn how to fight good, push them back, they no hurt you, yes?" the kid continued, offering Jamie a hand. "I can help you fight good. They leave me alone, see?"

Unlike the other children and now himself, Jamie realized that while there were some bruises on the boy's knuckles, he showed none on the rest of his body.

He finally nodded, extending his hand to grip the other boy's.

"I'm Jamie," he said, looking over to Sherry, who was starting to wake up. "And that's Sherry."

"My name is Santiago, but my friends call me Santa," the boy replied with a large smile, showing a missing tooth. "Nice to meet you. After breakfast we practice, okay?"

Jasper Joshua West

Chapter Five

SANTA WAS TRUE to his word, and Jamie found himself and Sherry spending more time with the boy. He had learned how to fight and speak English while spending most of his younger years on the streets of Cartagena; learning the language from tourists and fighting to keep others away from his food.

Jamie wasn't sure how the boy had managed on his own and was eager to learn. The fighting methods that Santa used weren't exactly fair, but neither were the methods used by the three boys who had attacked Jamie. They were all bigger and stronger than him, and he needed something of an edge.

Most of the training involved quick hits, since those were what Santa told him would win or lose a fight, and the rest involved moving out of the way. Jamie was quick on his feet, but Santa left him in the dust.

"You need to show pressure," Santa said, and when Jamie showed that he didn't understand, the boy continued. "You fight for life, so act like it. Every punch as hard as you can. Every move as fast as you can. You practice, you get better."

Jamie nodded, somewhat understanding the point.

One morning, a few days later, the men came over to Sherry, who was still in bed, telling her that she was going for a ride with them. Jamie wasn't sure what they had in mind, but the rude gesturing from the other boys was still vivid in his mind.

"If she's going somewhere, I'm going with her," Jamie said, standing up in front of the pair who had come to collect her.

Neither seemed sure about what to do, shaking their heads and talking between themselves. It was clear that neither wanted the trouble, and they quickly turned around, heading out of the room.

When they didn't come back, Jamie assumed that they had decided to not come for her.

***

One night when the lights went out, Jamie could see Juanito gathering his team again. They didn't look very happy about waking up, but it seemed they were going to try for Sherry and Jamie again.

But this time Jamie was ready for them. Quietly, and as subtly as possible, he wrapped two strips of cloth around his knuckles and pushed himself up as the boys reached their beds. This time four boys came.

They had been expecting the two to be asleep, but seemed undeterred, trying to climb onto Sherry's bed. One had almost reached his target and was fully exposed, so Jamie pounced on him. His fist lashed out with all the power that he could muster, hammering into the boy's stomach.

His breath left him in a rush, and he dropped to the ground with a thud.

The other boys reacted to the threat, but Jamie had taken Santa's advice to heart, immediately bringing his knee up to the groin of a second boy. Like the first, he dropped without a sound.

Juanito was left with just one of his gang, seeming almost unsure of what to do. Jamie took advantage of their hesitation. He grabbed Juanito by the neck and pulled him into the side of the bed, feeling the boy's head hit the wooden structure loudly and hard enough to leave a dent.

The last of Juanito's boys was trying to escape, and Jamie slipped in closer, tripping him up, causing him to land headfirst against another bedframe.

He could hear a noise coming from outside the door as the guards began responding to the commotion. Jamie turned to see Juanito trying to push himself up, looking dazed and slowed.

Jamie noticed a knife glinting in Juanito's hand.

Juanito put up little fight as Jamie yanked it from his numb fingers and tucked it into his own waistband, hiding it under his shirt. He deftly removed his knuckle wraps and hid them under his pillow. The guards turned the lights on and saw Jamie standing over the four boys.

"What happened?" one asked, looking at the four boys all beginning to recover.

"They fell," Jamie asserted confidently, looking down at Juanito. "Isn't that right?"

The boy paused, looking up at Jamie, rubbing his bruised face and nodded. "We fell."

It wasn't an outright lie, Jamie thought as the boys limped back toward their beds. He wondered if they would retaliate with even greater numbers the next time.

Chapter Six

THE STATE OF JUANITO and his gang was clear to everyone when morning dawned, and the happenings of the night before were quickly told and retold among them. Jamie wasn't sure of the reaction to expect from the group.

Afterwards, however, a few of the girls approached him to ask for protection from Juanito's gang, offering cigarettes as payment, but Jamie wasn't quite sure what to make of it.

"Just take them," Santa suggested when they were all in the mess hall for breakfast.

"But I don't smoke," Jamie pointed out. "I don't even like smoking. Where do they even get the cigarettes?"

"They're one of the few things that our guards allow inside," Santa replied. "And we're not allowed to have money. Sometimes the guards even give us smokes to keep us quiet, or if they want one of us to do something. A lot of us end up smoking them anyway, but they can also be used to buy other things, or pay people to do things."

"Do you smoke?" Jamie wondered.

"Sometimes," Santa said.

It seemed silly to turn down cigarettes. Besides, if he was going to be helping them, taking their cigarettes meant that they couldn't smoke them. He wasn't sure if he'd be able to use them for anything, but if he wasn't allowed to have money, at least they were something.

Some of the girls moved over to sleep in the bunk beds beside Jamie and Sherry's. Juanito and his gang didn't bother them for a while, but Jamie had a feeling that this would not be the last that he heard from them.

It was almost two weeks into their stay before the guards again came to take Sherry out on a trip, and this time they agreed to take Jamie along with her. The guards led them down to a car and, once inside, they were both blindfolded.

They drove for what seemed like hours. Despite being blindfolded, Jamie recognized the sounds and smells that only came from a city, and the car kept stopping and starting, which meant at least that they were still in Cartagena. They drove for almost a half hour before pulling into an underground garage, where they were taken into a hotel via the service elevator. If anyone saw them, there was no mention made of the two children being guided to a room on a high floor.

Two men who looked like foreign businessmen were waiting for them in the room. Jamie couldn't be sure where they were from but they spoke Spanish well and they didn't look American. The strangers smiled at Sherry and Jamie, but he couldn't help but feel creeped out by them.

One of the guards remained in the room, keeping an eye on Jamie and Sherry, who were pushed onto a sofa and told to wait as the second business man left the room with the other guards, closing the door behind them.

"Can I get you kids something to drink?" the remaining man asked in a soft voice. "A beer, maybe?"

Jamie shook his head but didn't say anything. He was thirsty but he didn't want anything from this man. He wondered if he would be able to punch his way through this as he had with Juanito's group. He doubted it, but he would have to try if they made to hurt Sherry.

The man shrugged, leaning back in his seat. "It'll help you relax; I'll tell you that much."

Jamie clenched his jaw again, and didn't answer as the door opened again and the other adults returned. The businessman looked angry. He turned to address his partner and in a foreign language as the guards pulled the two children from the room and back down to the car.

They probably hadn't come to an agreement on a price, Jamie told Sherry as they were again blindfolded. It was unlikely that the guards cared about what would have been in store for him and Sherry had they been left behind in that hotel room.

He felt sick to his stomach, but he held the feeling in until they were back at what they thought of as home. As soon as they got back upstairs, Jamie found his way to the bathroom and threw up. He told himself it was from riding in the car being blindfolded, but it was probably more to do with the disgust of thinking about what the two strangers had wanted from him and Sherry.

Chapter Seven

IT WAS ONE of those nights where Jamie found his eyes starting to close almost as soon as the lights went off and his head hit the pillow. He hadn't been getting much sleep, worrying about Juanito's gang coming to them in the night, and it was catching up to him. He began to think they might not bother him and Sherry anymore.

He couldn't tell how long he'd been asleep. It could've been a few minutes, or a few hours, there was no telling.

All he knew was that he was instantly awake, looking up into the eyes of Juanito in the darkness of the room. Hands were gripping and pinning his hands above his head. All four were back, and this time they would not be denied.

Two boys were pinning Jamie down, with Juanito holding Jamie's knife to his neck. Two other boys climbed up to the top bunk bed where Sherry lay.

He could hear soft cries of surprise from Sherry muffled likely by the boy's hand, and Jamie could feel a fire in his veins suddenly taking over. He bucked against the grip on his hands and shoulders, fighting to get free.

Juanito paused, pulling the knife from Jamie's throat, showing he had no intention of killing him. It was a moment of weakness, even if the hand was moving up to help contain Jamie, and it was one that he wasn't going to forgive.

Jamie struggled to get his hands free, then he used their distraction to draw attention from his legs, and his knee shot up and hammered Juanito in the temple.

Pain seared across Jamie's arm. He hadn't seen it happen, but he knew instinctively Juanito had cut him. At least it was his arm and not his throat, he thought. Jamie's right hand was free, and his thumb moved up to the eye of the boy closest to him, and he pushed as hard as he could with a loud grunt.

"*Mierda!*" the boy shouted, falling away as Jamie found his arms free again, jerking them away.

One boy remained close to him, looking panicked as Jamie jumped from his bed, screaming and gripping at the boy's throat. Jamie took the boys head in both of his hands and smashed it into the floor as hard as he could. The boy went limp.

Jamie was on his feet again, turning and jumping up to the top bunk as the lights came on. The boys had already torn Sherry's clothes and one of them had climbed on top of her.

Jamie gripped him by the shoulder and rolled them both off of the bed, to land heavily on the floor.

"Stay away from her!" Jamie screamed, recovering quickly despite the pain in his arm. He threw a few hard punches at the boy's head and his stomach before straddling his chest.

Before Jamie could throw anymore punches, he was dragged away from the boy. He managed to kick the boy in the face as he was drug away, leaving the boy limp on the ground.

"Enough *niño,*" shouted the guard pulling Jamie off, and pushing him back onto his bed.

What Juanito's boys had been doing wasn't lost on the men, and Jamie watched from his bed as two boys were dragged from the room, nursing their wounds as Jamie used a knuckle wrap to bandage the cut on his arm.

He saw that Juanito had abandoned the knife on the bed, likely dropping it when he'd been kneed in the head. Jamie kept his eye on the boy who had been ignored by the two guards as he returned to his bed. The boy didn't look up and didn't notice Jamie watching him like a hawk with fire in his eyes as the lights went out again.

Chapter Eight

JAMIE COULDN'T SLEEP, but he was getting used to that. The guards managed to get Sherry fresh clothes, but she clung to his side the whole next day. An indication that the events of the night before was still on her mind. Jamie felt bad that she had been scared, but he was glad that the boys hadn't had the chance to actually hurt her as they had no doubt intended to do.

Jamie needed to do something; just defending himself and Sherry would end badly for him. He had been lucky to get a hit in before anything happened to Sherry this time, but there was no guarantee that he would be able to do that again.

A message needed to be sent. The whole night and day Jamie could feel something hot in his chest and stomach, thinking of the way Juanito had looked down at him in the darkness.

Jamie clenched his jaw as the lights went out again the next night, waiting until he could hear the shallow breathing from the bunk bed above him which told him that Sherry had fallen asleep.

Jamie climbed out of his bed, feeling his heart thudding hard in his chest as he pulled the knife out from under his mattress. He moved over to the bunks occupied by Juanito and his gang, keeping himself low. He wasn't sure what had happened to the boys that had been caught trying to hurt Sherry, but they hadn't been around since then. Now it was just Juanito and one other bad boy.

It wasn't that Jamie felt confident, he just was no longer prepared to be afraid of the bully. He gripped the knife in his hand a little tighter as he moved in next to Juanito's bed, trying move silently as he approached.

Juanito was sound asleep, but his eyes jerked open as Jamie placed his hand over his mouth. He reached up to resist but stopped when he felt the knife pressed to his neck.

Jamie had vowed to himself that he would kill Juanito. He had pictured it all day and imagined what it would look like when he did.

But as he stood over Juanito, looking at the sheer terror in his eyes, reflected in the meager light of the bunk room, Jamie didn't think he could do it. The boy was a bully, and terrible, but killing him just didn't feel right. Besides, he didn't know if the guards would punish him for killing another boy, and he didn't want to risk being separated from Sherry.

Jamie scowled, pressing the knife a little tighter to Juanito's neck before he pulled away, deciding that he wasn't going to go through with his murderous intent.

But a message still needed to be sent. Jamie looked down to find that the wound on his arm had reopened with the improvised bandage absorbing the blood.

Juanito's eyes looked over to the wound as well, and then to the knife. This gave Jamie an idea. He slowly moved the knife over to the other boy's arm, his terrified eyes watching in the gloom. When he tried to move his arm, Jamie pinned it down with his knee, holding it in place as he dragged the blade across Juanito's bicep in the same way that it had cut Jamie's arm a few nights ago.

The muffled cries were almost inaudible, not waking anyone as Jamie pulled back, leaving the cut as a visible reminder for all the boys of what would happen if any further attempts were made to attack him or Sherry.

Jasper Joshua West

Second Hand

Chapter Nine

THERE WERE NO consequences for Juanito's injured arm. Jamie had hoped there wouldn't be, but he was still surprised to be left alone from that point forward, by the guards as well as the other boys. Juanito bandaged his injured arm. The other members of his gang barely even spoke out again.

Jamie knew that wasn't likely to be the end of it, but for now something calming came over him. He was able to sleep a little better, although the many nightmares he couldn't remember often woke him.

The children were separated as usual for showers, and the boys mostly seemed content to leave Jamie alone. Even when he didn't have his knife on him, none of them were willing to come up against him.

It was an odd feeling. Jamie knew for a fact that the others were stronger than he was. Santa seemed just as scared of him as the others were, and Jamie knew that the kid could beat him black and blue if he wanted to.

They all stayed away from him, though, as if they were afraid of him. Jamie wasn't sure if he liked that, but in the end, if it kept them away from Sherry, he would take it.

Jamie finished showering, drying himself off with a towel provided and got back into his clothes as everybody was making their way back to their rooms. Sherry usually tried to find him after the showers, but she was nowhere to be seen.

Jamie asked a few of the other girls if they had seen her but they didn't respond, just looking away from Jamie. He suddenly knew something was wrong. The two guards who usually kept an eye on the group of children were also missing.

Jamie rushed to the bunks and grabbed the knife that he had hidden in his bed, pushing kids out of his way without a second thought. The guards had gotten their hands on Sherry, and he wasn't going to let them get away with that, not if they were taking her for a ride.

Jamie was already running down the steps before he could even think about what he was doing, or what he was going to do when he caught up to them.

As he reached the ground floor, entering a well-lit hallway, Jamie could see two men walking Sherry towards the exit holding her up by her shoulders.

"What is he doing here?" one of the men said in Spanish when he spotted Jamie.

"Leave her alone!" Jamie said, rushing towards them. Two other men stepped into his view, blocking his way to Sherry.

Jamie still didn't know what he was going to do, but he needed to get to the door before they took her out. Hands reached out for his shoulders, and Jamie tried to pull away from them but when they clamped down and stopped him.

Jamie drew upon the skills that Santa had drilled into him. His hand, clenched in a fist, hammered into the groin of the man on the right. The man grunted in pain, doubling over as Jamie's elbow hit the second man's stomach, right where Santa had taught him to hit. The breath rushed from the man's lungs and he too dropped to the ground.

"Sherry!" Jamie shouted, running after her as the door closed between them. Jamie wrenched open the door and ran out.

A man escorting Sherry turned around, and found Jamie charging at them. They weren't going to let him go with her, not this time. If that were the plan, they would have just pulled them both instead of resorting to trickery.

The man scowled. His fist came up, and Jamie tried to dodge it. He almost did. The punch sailed a little high but clipped him right behind the ear and Jamie hit the ground. The world was spinning, and he could feel his stomach churning.

But he was still awake.

"*Vámonos,*" the man snapped and pulled Sherry toward a car.

Chapter Ten

JAMIE PUSHED HIMSELF up off the ground. The hit hadn't knocked him out, as he thought it would, but the world was still spinning. It got worse when he got to his feet; little flickers of light jumped around in front of his eyes as he struggled to stay on his feet.

But he fought it off. Sherry hadn't gotten too far.

His stomach threatened to hurl again, but Jamie leaned against the door, fighting it back, shaking his head gently; that didn't help. He stopped moving, taking long deep breaths to keep himself awake. It didn't work but did some good when he finally spotted Sherry and ran toward her.

They dragged Sherry, over to one of the parked cars. One of the men walked ahead of the other two, pulling a set of keys from his pocket and pressing a button which caused the car's lights to flash and emitted a tone of three soft chirps. This told Jamie that the alarm was turned off and the car was unlocked.

The man taking the lead opened the back door of the car and proceeded to the driver's seat to start the engine.

Jamie wasn't sure how he was able to run when only seconds before he had struggled to stay on his feet. Putting one foot in front of the other, he began picking up speed. His heart was pounding, and there was a dull ache in the back of his head where he had been punched, but that didn't stop him from running as fast as he could.

He tripped on the uneven ground, but still managed to close in on the men as they pushed Sherry into the car. Sherry fell over onto the seat, possibly asleep.

"No!" Jamie shouted, pulling the knife from his pocket. This caught the attention of the man who had closed the car door on Sherry to turn and see Jamie charging at him.

He had no time to throw a punch this time and Jamie was on him before he could react. Jamie head-butted the man in the stomach, which was enough to double the man over, but Jamie also went sprawling to the ground.

As Jamie recovered and quickly got to his feet, he looked around, suddenly not seeing Sherry. He shook his head to clear it and looked in the car. It hadn't moved yet, but the lights flickered on and then shuddered as the sound of the car's engine echoed in the garage.

"No!" Jamie shouted again. He wasn't sure why he was yelling. His throat was sore and the pounding in his head was getting worse, but Sherry was getting away. The car started fully this time, coughing out a cloud of foul-smelling smoke as Jamie ran toward it.

The world twisted and swam around him, but he reached out for the car door, pulling it open just as it started moving.

Second Hand

Chapter Eleven

THE CAR ACCELERATED toward the exit despite Jamie having the door open. Jamie was barely able to dive into the back seat beside Sherry as the car picked up speed, tires squealing and engine roaring.

Jamie was knocked out of the seat and onto the floor as they hit the ramp out of the garage going too fast. The open door struck one of the pillars, breaking the glass and bending the door frame which caused the door to remain open as they drove out into the street.

Jamie looked around the floor of the car, feeling for the knife that had fallen from his hands. He finally found it and sat back in the seat for a moment trying to catch his breath. The driver was driving madly and didn't pay any attention to Jamie.

"Are you okay," Jamie asked Sherry.

Sherry looked at him with tears in her eyes and nodded. She didn't appear to be physically hurt but she was terrified. Jamie put an arm around her and held her tight.

The car continued moving for a few long minutes until it screeched to a halt again, hammering Jamie against the front seat, and leaving him in an uncomfortable pile on the floor of the back seat.

"No se mueven!" *Don't move!* the man shouted, and Jamie looked up to see a gun pointed at Sherry.

The man cursed softly and pulled a phone from his pocket, the gun faltering so Jamie noticed it now pointed over their heads. He dialed a number and put the phone to his ear.

Someone answered the man's call, and they got to the point quickly. Jamie could hear the excited shouts on the other end of the line. They were talking Spanish, but maybe through desperation, Jamie could understand what they were saying.

"Kill the boy, take the girl to the drop off," he heard the person on the other end say.

They were going to kill him and leave Sherry all alone in this world, without anyone to help her.

That fire in his stomach started up again, his heart thudding and ticking loudly in his chest as Jamie surged off the floor and into the front seat. The man's gun hand was caught on Jamie's shoulder, and he pushed it upwards as the man pulled the trigger.

The sound of the gunshot in his ear deafened him, but he didn't stop. Jamie pushed the knife into the driver's face and was cutting at anything he could find. His ears were ringing, but he sensed the man's screams as the knife cut into his throat, opening it up. Blood spurted out, coating Jamie's arms and neck.

Another short rang out, but the light faded from the driver's eyes and he dropped back against his seat, body slack and the smoking gun dropping from his lifeless fingers.

Jamie's eyes were tearing up, his ears still ringing as he pulled his knife from the man's neck.

Jamie turned to look at Sherry who had come to and was staring at him with wide eyes.

"Are you okay?" Sherry asked him. Jamie's ears were ringing but he could read the words on her lips.

He nodded slowly. Physically, he was okay, but he had just killed a man. That changed a person. But there wasn't time to worry about that now. He could hear sirens in the distance and knew they had to get away from the car.

Jamie moved down, picking the gun up from where it had fallen on the floor, tucking it and his knife into his pockets before climbing into the back seat.

"Come on, we're getting out of here," Jamie said, tugging Sherry's hand to open the door.

"Oh my God!" she said, her voice slurring as they climbed out of the car. "You're bleeding."

Jamie checked himself quickly. He was hurting and aching, but there was no sign of injury.

"I'm fine," Jamie said. "It's not my blood. Let's go."

They jumped out of the car and ran into the night as the sirens grew louder.

Chapter Twelve

JAMIE AND SHERRY walked through the back streets of the city. They didn't run into too many people, and those they did tried to stay away from them. Jamie didn't blame them; he could imagine how they looked, bruised and covered in blood.

Jamie wasn't sure if that was good or bad, but it sure did simplify matters. Maybe folks in the city of Cartagena were used to the sight of kids covered in blood.

As they walked, the shock wore off and Sherry finally started crying. Not loudly, but rather involuntarily. Jamie would have wrapped his arms around her but figured she wouldn't want the blood on her from his hands, arms, and chest.

Moving through the streets, Jamie finally found a small park that looked to be deserted at this time of day. He saw no hoses or water fountains, but there was a small lake.

Jamie led Sherry over to the water. He could feel the blood becoming sticky on his skin.

They reached the water and without speaking a word to each other, Jamie cleaned Sherry of the blood splatter from the earlier struggle in the car. He hadn't been sure of what to do with the gun, but after a few seconds of tinkering, he managed to remove the cylinder from the revolver.

There were no more bullets, which was a little annoying, but Jamie wasn't sure what he would do with a loaded gun anyway. His ears were still ringing as he crouched by the waterside to wash the blood from his hands.

There was a lot of blood, and it was difficult to get it all off, especially from his clothes. Every time he looked at his hands to check if they were clean, images of the knife plunging into the man's throat flashed through his mind. That reminded him to wash off the knife too. His shirt and shorts were probably stained beyond washing.

"What are we going to do now?" Sherry asked, her voice sounding a little raw as she sat down next to him.

Jamie stared down at his hands, taking slow, deep breaths, trying to calm himself even as he wondered the same.

"I don't know," Jamie finally admitted, hearing police sirens approaching. "We'll figure it out, though."

Chapter Thirteen

JAMIE COULDN'T GET the blood out of his clothes. He stopped trying after an hour of scrubbing. The best he managed was a dull pink that had spread through the fabric.

Jamie dropped to the ground next to Sherry, shaking his head. His ears were still ringing, and he had aches and pains all over. His fingers were aching, but he wasn't sure why, which was also the case with other bruises here and there, but overall, he just felt tired.

"Thanks," Sherry mumbled softly. "For… you know, everything."

Jamie shook his head. "Nothing you wouldn't do for me."

She nodded. "Still though. How old are you?"

Jamie looked up at the odd question. They had been together for over a year now. He just assumed that she knew how old he was, but then he realized that they hadn't actually discussed it. Nor did he know much about her.

"I'm eleven, I think," Jamie said. "I was almost ten when they took me from my school, and it's been more than a year.. I'm not sure how long it's been since then, exactly, but I think it's been more than a year."

"They took me when I was walking home from school," Sherry replied, running her fingers through her tangled hair. "I think you're right. It's been more than a year. So I must be ten now."

Jamie nodded. It was difficult to keep track of the length of time they had been captive. It wasn't as if they had calendars or watches.

"Do you think we'll ever get home?" Sherry asked, looking to Jamie.

He was torn. Jamie could tell that she was looking for comfort, something that would help to keep her spirits up. They had escaped the men holding them captive, but that resulted in no food, no resources and no way to get home that Jamie could think of. He didn't even know how they had come to be here in the first place.

On the one hand, he wanted to say that they were going to get out, find their families and head home now that they were free. But he wasn't sure he believed that anymore. Dan, and Sam were gone. Everyone was gone, except Sherry.

Sam said their parents were killed, but he didn't want to tell Sherry that. He trusted Sam, but something about the story didn't seem right, and he preferred not talking about it with anyone. As long as no one else knew, he could pretend it wasn't true.

"I hope so," Jamie finally said, forcing a smile. "We need to get out of here."

Sherry looked over to where his eyes had suddenly shifted. There were families, mothers with small children, coming into view. Citizens that would likely not take too well to seeing two bloodstained children interrupting their happy afternoon.

"Let's go," she agreed.

Jasper Joshua West

Chapter Fourteen

JAMIE WASN'T MUCH GOOD at shoplifting. There was no school or training that could teach him how, but they had no food or water, and they weren't going to survive without it. He wished they'd drank from the lake before they left, but that was no longer an option.

The thought of using the gun to rob a shop for food did occur to him, but if they ever pushed him to use it, he wouldn't be able to. And then he would be arrested for threatening people with a gun.

It was better to just take what he could when people weren't looking, and keep the gun hidden in case he got caught and needed to scare someone with it. That way he could run with what he had without attracting too much attention.

A small convenience store had a refrigerator outside stocked with large bottles of water. Jamie bided his time, waiting for the shop owner to busy himself tending to customers before moving forward, pulling the door open and taking two bottles of water before running away.

He didn't know whether or not the owner had seen him, but nobody shouted or made any trouble as he rounded the corner to join the waiting Sherry.

"Did you get any food?" Sherry asked, but her face fell as all she saw in his hands was the water.

"This was all I could grab," Jamie said, handing her one of the bottles, cool and dripping with condensation.

It wasn't much but it would do for now, as Sherry quickly peeled the top off and took a long drink from the cool bottle of water. It was a hot day; hotter when they were out in the heat, on their own, on their feet and running.

"We have to find a place to spend the night," Jamie said, wiping his face on his sleeve.

"Maybe we can go back to the park?" she asked. "It was nice there."

Jamie shook his head. "I saw police patrolling the area. I think they're there to kick out homeless people. That's what we are now: homeless. We need to find somewhere else."

"Hey, you two!"

Jamie turned around, his hand moving around to the gun that he had hidden in his back pocket.

Two men were standing at the edge of their sidewalk, dressed like tourists. They were speaking between themselves in a language that Jamie didn't understand.

"What... what?" Jamie asked.

"I saw... you steal from the store," one man said, and immediately raised his hands. "I no take you to police. But I buy you and girl some food, and I pay for the water too, okay? Just... I go into the store, and I buy, is that okay?"

Jamie didn't want to trust the man, but the growl in his stomach reminded him that they hadn't eaten all day, not at all since they had run away. Food, no matter the source, was sounded appealing now.

"Okay," Jamie said.

The men walked away and returned a few minutes later with a couple of empanadas, a bag of chips and more water.

"Thank you," Sherry said softly, taking the food from their hands.

The men smiled, speaking more of the language that Jamie couldn't understand, and went on their way. Jamie and Sherry dug in and made short work of the food.

"Wow that was good," Jamie said with a small smile. "Let's find somewhere to sleep now."

Chapter Fifteen

JAMIE JUMPED UP, roused from sleep instantly. His head struck the low roof covering the back of the battered little Toyota pickup truck where they slept.

"Ouch," Jamie whispered, rubbing his head. He turned to see that he'd woken Sherry. The shelter, such as it was, was better than sleeping out in the open, barely.

"What's the matter?" Sherry whispered.

Jamie looked around for the source of the noise that had woken him, then spotted it.

"The people in that house," Jamie said. "They're awake. Maybe they're coming out soon. Come on."

He took her by the hand, guiding her out of the pickup and into one of the alleyways that they had been skulking through.

"I'm still tired," Sherry complained.

Jamie nodded. "Put your head on my shoulder."

They both sat down on the ground, and Sherry leaned into his shoulder, quickly falling asleep again as he wrapped his arm around her. It wasn't the most comfortable way to sleep, but if they were going to get a couple more hours of sleep then they needed to do so before the heat of the day made sleeping outside impossible. He settled into place, letting Sherry settle a bit more as he watched the owners of the house come out and drive away in the yellow pickup truck, leaving a trail of black smoke.

It wasn't long before they needed to move again; more people were moving through the street, and these people, the locals, did not look friendly like the tourists had.

They reached a small outdoor restaurant, where the owners would not allow them entry, but a couple of tourists took pity on them and bought them food to eat. A police car came along and the officer started shouting at them. Jamie gripped Sherry's hand and together they ran off, taking the food that they had been given with them.

"Why didn't we talk to the police?" Sherry asked when they finally stopped, out of breath. "They can help us, right?"

"Right," Jamie said, nodding. "Or they can be like those cops that took money from Sam. You remember the ones that showed up outside the camp when we met. If we run into the wrong one, they might turn us back over to those… people, and since we – I killed that guy, they won't… They'll kill me. And even if we run into one of the honest cops, they might know that we were involved in killing that guy. That means prison, or maybe worse."

She nodded, tears running down her cheeks. "You know we can't run forever, right? We won't be able to get back home on our own!"

Jamie scowled. "I know!"

"What's your plan?" she shouted at him. "Do you have a plan to get us home? You don't, do you?"

Jamie clenched his jaw, trying to keep the threatening tears from falling from his eyes as Sherry turned around and stormed out of the alleyway.

Jasper Joshua West

Chapter Sixteen

SHERRY WAS ANGRY so Jamie gave her some space. They had both been through enough together as it was, and maybe she just needed a moment or two to gather herself before coming back.

Jamie still followed her as she started wandering the streets, running away for a few blocks before slowing down to a walk. Jamie kept his distance, but still kept her in sight. He still felt responsible for keeping her safe, even if she had apparently lost her faith in his ability to do so.

If he was being honest with himself, Jamie had abandoned all hope of getting back home, and therefore had no plan aside from surviving as long as possible. Maybe her parents would still be looking for her, and someone would recognize her and send her home. But for him it was different; he'd been gone for much longer.

It was likely that people back home thought he was dead.

Jamie shook his head at the thought, moving forward as Sherry approached what looked like a bus stop, just as a bus was arriving. A large group of people disembarked, including vendors with their produce, slung over their backs from a stick. These were all# locals, though, since most of the tourists tended to use taxis.

"Damn it," Jamie growled, losing sight of Sherry in the crowd. His heart started pounding a little harder as he picked up his pace, looking around the group. If he saw her, he would be able to pick her out instantly, but there were so many adults around him that it was impossible to see through the group.

They moved quickly, mostly ignoring Jamie as a street urchin. A few of the older women clutched their purses and belongings a little closer, expecting that he might try to pick their pockets, but Jamie passed them by without so much as a glance.

She wasn't no longer on the street. Had she seen him following her and taken advantage of the distraction to run away?

No, that didn't seem like her.

Jamie moved quickly, retracing his steps, feeling the panic starting to well up in his chest until he found a small one-way street that they usually used to hide in.

She was sitting on the sidewalk, face in her hands, and sobbing.

Jamie moved in and sat down next to her, not saying a word. He didn't know what to say to help, and all he could really do was be there with her.

"I'm sorry," she finally said, her voice cracking as she gripped his hand again. "It's… I'm hungry, and thirsty, and tired. I don't know how… I…"

"It's okay," Jamie mumbled, hugging her and letting her sob into his shirt. He could feel her tears through the fabric, but he didn't really mind.

He was only happy that he hadn't lost her.

The faint rumble of thunder had his eyes turn upwards towards the sky where he could see the clouds starting to darken above them.

"I think we better get moving," he said, patting the top of Sherry's head. "I don't think we want to get caught out in a rainstorm like this."

Chapter Seventeen

THE STREETS GREW even more hectic when the rain started coming down, and it wasn't long before they were both splashed with mud and soaked through. Getting off the streets seemed to be a priority, and they found a park in the city where Jamie could see a small gazebo at the top of a hill.

Sherry and Jamie both moved inside. Despite the warm weather, the rain was still cold enough to chill them to the bone, and they stayed inside for a while to warm up. It was hot enough inside that the cold quickly passed.

It wasn't long, however, before Jamie saw a few local kids about their age playing in the rain in their underwear. They ran up to the top of the, dragging big pieces of cardboard behind them. Once at the top, one would climb on and slide all the way down the hill. Some younger kids joined them, stripping off their clothes and sliding down the hill on their bottoms. Sometimes the other kids would make a wrong turn and the sled would turn over, but then the children would continue sliding or rolling down the hill on their own, laughing as they did.

For a moment, Jamie couldn't help a small wish to be one of those kids instead of living on the street. He didn't like the feeling, and quickly pushed it to the back of his mind. Sherry was standing at the window, watching them.

"Do you want to go out there to play with them?" he asked.

She shrugged her shoulders. "I don't know. Could be fun, I guess."

"We'll get wet," Jamie pointed out.

"We're already wet, and it looks like they're having fun," Sherry insisted. "Come on, don't you want to go out and have some fun?"

Some fun? An odd concept, so long absent from his life. The thought made an odd smile come to his face.

"Sure, why not?" he finally replied.

"Yes," she hissed, running out of the gazebo, and rushing out into the rain that they had been avoiding only fifteen minutes ago. Jamie smiled as Sherry talked one of the girls into letting her use the makeshift sled. The other children pushed her over the hill and she slid all the way down, skidding across the puddles that were starting to form at the bottom.

Jamie couldn't help a small smile as he ran down to help her bring the sled up.

"Do you want a turn?" Sherry asked.

"No, you go again," Jamie said with a laugh, this time helping the children push her. "You keep going until you tip over, that's the rule."

She was halfway down when the sled overturned, throwing her head over heels the rest of the way down. Jamie's worry over her being hurt quickly fell away as she pushed back up to her feet, laughing and pulling the sled back up the hill.

It was nice to see her laughing again. Jamie didn't think he would ever see that again.

He hoped it would last.

Jasper Joshua West

Chapter Eighteen

THEY WERE STILL HOMELESS in a foreign country, but Jamie tried to forget about that as they played. One of the other boys gestured for Jamie to take off his shirt and hang it with the clothes the local kids and hung over a fence at the bottom of the hill. He obliged and when realized how good the rain felt against his bare skin, he took off his shorts too.

Once the rain stopped, the children all had somewhere to go, probably inside to dry off and warm up. Sherry and Jamie, who had been having fun until that point, were saddened by the reminder that they didn't have anywhere to go. They began wandering again and eventually made their way to a small abandoned warehouse where they hung their clothes up to dry and Jamie laid down to rest on some old canvas bags.

"That was fun," Sherry said as she straightened their clothes on the improvised line. "Been a while since…"

She didn't need to say it aloud, and Jamie nodded in agreement. It had been a while, but he wasn't going to keep dwelling on it. The warehouse that they'd picked was abandoned for the moment but there were people working nearby.

Sherry didn't seem worried about that, however. The sun came out from behind the clouds and shone down on them bright and warm. Sherry laid down next to Jamie and yawned. They hadn't slept much the night before and it wasn't long before they both fell asleep.

***

It could have been hours or minutes that passed, but the sound of shouting around them got Jamie on to his feet quickly. A group of men were yelling, seemingly having arrived at work to find Sherry and Jamie in their way.

At least their clothes were dry; they got dressed quickly, running out of the door that one of the men was holding open for them.

"They seemed nice enough," Sherry noted in passing when they came to a halt.

"They were yelling at us to leave."

"Sure, but they could have been a lot meaner about it. They just wanted to get back to work, I think."

Jamie shrugged his shoulders. It was nice that Sherry was still able to think about the needs and wants of others. He found that all he could be worried about was what was happening to them.

"Let's go," Jamie said, nudging her shoulder gently as a large group of tourists came into view all heading into town, taking pictures. This was their chance.

The tourists were the most giving and generous, with the fewest questions. Locals tended to be a little thriftier, suspecting children wandering around their town as pickpockets and thieves. There wasn't much that they could say to change their minds.

Jamie smiled as a couple of notes and coins were pressed into their hands. Sherry was having better luck. She looked younger, and the fact that she was a girl made them feel a little better about giving her money. Jamie didn't mind, knowing that she would share the money with him anyway.

"Hey, you two, where are you from?" one of the men asked in a strange accent.

Sherry answered before Jamie could. "I'm from Canada, he's from the US. We were kidnapped and brought down here, and we're trying to get back home."

The man laughed. Jamie narrowed his eyes, seeing that they didn't believe her. They considered it to be either a joke or just another sob story to get more money. The rest of the tourists moved away quickly.

"Why don't they believe us?" Sherry asked.

Jamie shrugged. "I don't know. Maybe they just don't want to. At least we have some money for food tonight."

Chapter Nineteen

"WE NEED TO GET OUT OF HERE," Jamie said.

Sherry looked around, turning from the meal that they had just purchased from a street vendor. They were getting used to the spicy food common in this country by now, but it still left Jamie sweating.

"What?" she asked. "I'm not finished yet."

Jamie pointed towards one of the nearby hotels. He could see a security man walking over to a police car that had just pulled up. He was talking to the officers and pointing to Sherry and him. Jamie noticed then that the other beggars usually in the area had all vanished. They knew better than to deal with the cops.

"Maybe they can help us?" Sherry insisted, finishing her food and tossing the wrappers.

"I don't think so," Jamie said. "Come on, we need to…"

He froze as he saw another car pull up, cutting off their escape. Two officers quickly walked up to Jamie and Sherry, placing a hand on their shoulders, keeping them in place.

They spoke in Spanish, asking what the two children were doing there.

"We were kidnapped," Sherry insisted in English. "They took us from our homes and brought us here. Why can't you just help us to contact our parents?"

The officers either didn't understand or didn't believe them. Jamie kept as compliant as possible, giving Sherry's hand one last squeeze before they were pushed into the police car. The officers didn't look happy about having the dirty children in their back seat, but they said no more as they started the car.

"Do you think they're taking us to the police station?" Sherry whispered.

Jamie clenched his teeth, trying his best to keep a positive mindset. "I heard them say something about taking us back where we belong."

"I guess… that's not the police station then?"

He shook his head. "I don't think so."

Sure enough, he saw no sign of a station in the area. They were heading into one of the slums of the city which as they slowed down, appeared the kind of place where they would not be causing any trouble.

It didn't look safe, but then again, neither had any of the places they'd been. Jamie could only guess that these people were going to do a lot more than yell and call the police. They needed to be more careful now.

The officers pulled them out of the car roughly and without another word, slammed their doors and drove off. The message was clear: stay out of the nice part of town.

Jamie didn't know what else they could do, but he wasn't going to push them. At least they hadn't bothered to search him. He still had the empty gun, his knife and a little money left over after buying their lunch.

"Why won't anyone help us?" Sherry asked, and Jamie saw that she was trying not to cry.

"They will," Jamie assured her, helping her back to her feet. "Eventually. Someone's got to."

He wasn't sure if he believed that, but it was a nice thought.

Jasper Joshua West

Chapter Twenty

THERE WERE A LOT more people on the streets in this area, but none of them were tourists. A lot of them were children, dirty and dressed in rags, or in the case of some of the younger children, not dressed at all. Adults wandered the streets or sat in abandoned buildings.

Not knowing what else to do, Jamie and Sherry walked toward a bus station where they saw some local kids outside begging. When they got closer, they saw they weren't just begging, though. Some were also pickpocketing. Jamie watched as one child shouted, attracting the attention of people passing by as their friends moved in behind grabbing whatever they could from pockets and purses. It reminded Jamie of Oliver Twist, only most times the children didn't get anything, and they often had to run away when people caught them trying to pick their pockets.

There were shacks put up with makeshift materials, mostly pieces of wood and aluminum, with chunks of rock and concrete put in here or there. Wiring from inside the buildings provided lit up a few scattered light bulbs which flickered.

Jamie had never seen such a place. People who were all in the same boat as him and Sherry or worse off. He gripped her hand, keeping their meager belongings close, as they moved through the groups.

One of the children saw Jamie and Sherry sticking together, and approached them cautiously, speaking Spanish. He was about Jamie's age and he had long, unruly dark hair. He was filthy and he wore only a tattered pair of shorts and sandals made from plastic bottles. He carried a plastic bag with more bottles and cans in it.

"What's he saying?" Sherry whispered.

"He's asking if we have somewhere to sleep," Jamie said, and turned to the boy. "Non," he said, and shook his head.

The child indicated for them to follow him. The sun was setting so Jamie and Sherry followed the boy through the streets towards a section where he could see a group of children starting to settle in for the night.

"Seems like the kids around here stick together," Jamie noted as they joined the ad hoc little town of homeless children.

"That's nice," Sherry said, yawning. What seemed to be social workers came around to them, serving disposable bowls of soup and slices of cheap white bread to the children. Sherry and Jamie tried to explain where they were from again, but from the awkward smiles of the women dressed like nuns, he could see that they didn't understand what was being said.

"Just our luck, I guess," Jamie grumbled.

"We have food," Sherry said softly, turning to look up at Jamie. "We have a place to sleep."

"Probably want to keep a hand and an eye on what we do have."

Sherry smiled and leaned against his shoulder. Jamie could hear her breathing starting to slow and deepen. Even with the nap that they'd had earlier in the day, it had been a long day with not enough sleep.

Jamie looked around at the homeless people and was once again reminded that him and Sherry were also homeless. These people all had about as much as they did or less, but there was something wholesome about how they were willing to share what little they had with two strangers.

If nothing else, it showed that while the rich in the city disliked having poor people around, those that had less were more willing to show their more human side.

The sky darkened as the sun dropped out of sight. The nuns were handing out blankets, and Jamie claimed one for himself and Sherry as they settled in for the night. Thankfully, the heat of the day didn't dissipate quickly in the humidity, so it wasn't cold at all, which allowed Jamie to lean back against one of the shacks, and drift off to sleep.

Chapter Twenty-One

MORNING CAME ALONG quickly, and Jamie found himself actually feeling more rested than he'd felt in a while. Almost impossibly, he thought.

The rest of the children were up with the sun and a quick nudge from them had Jamie and Sherry up off the ground too. The nuns weren't coming back to collect the blankets, so Sherry, who looked a little more tired than usual, kept the one they had wrapped around her shoulders, as they followed the group of children heading towards the streets.

Some looked like they were going right to work, but the one that had directed Jamie and Sherry indicated for them to follow him. Jamie was fairly suspicious of the child's goodwill, but as a larger group of about a dozen children joined them, he relaxed a little.

Besides, with his knife and the gun, he could probably scare people long enough to run away if things got ugly.

They came to a halt outside of what looked and smelled like a restaurant, or maybe a bakery. The children sat down and waited as if this was a normal routine and so Jamie indicated for Sherry to do the same.

After about fifteen minutes of waiting, the nearby door opened, and a thick set man walked out carrying a couple of black trash bags. Instead of tossing them into the trash bins, he left them at the foot of the steps.

The children approached the bags, opening them to expose a treasure of bread and pastries. The flour dusting suggested that the bread was probably stale and old, likely having not been sold over the past few days. However, it was still food, and better than what he could probably expect to buy with what little cash they still had.

Jamie picked out a couple of smaller loaves and one of the pastries stuffed with mango jam, and handed them to Sherry, who quickly wolfed them down. She spilled a little of the jam on the ground but didn't appear to mind. Jamie grabbed up a couple of pastries and began eating too.

"See?" Sherry asked, wiping the crumbs from her mouth and smiling. "Things could definitely be worse. When was the last time you remember getting two square meals one after the other?"

Not since they had left their captors, but Jamie didn't want to say that out loud. They still needed to find some way to get food and shelter, and he only wanted them to worry about one thing at a time.

They didn't want to return to the tourist area, but the transportation areas in the slums were picked dry. A couple of the larger children, and a couple of grownups along with them shouted for Jamie and Sherry not to intrude on their territory. While others made sure that neither were going to be able to sleep in some abandoned shacks that they found, forcing Jamie and Sherry back to the spot that they had spent the night before. The nuns were back, giving out soup and bread and blankets.

And once again, they were set to spend the night under the stars, with Sherry curled up beside him, mumbling softly in her sleep.

Jamie couldn't help a small smile. They didn't quite have a full belly, but at least they weren't starving. It wasn't a permanent solution for them, of course, but it would do for now.

One problem at a time.

Jasper Joshua West

Chapter Twenty-Two

IT WAS MORE of the same the next day.

Jamie and Sherry ended up finding their way to a bigger bus stations where fewer gangs were at work, with more police presence, but they still didn't have much success. Having to get around quicker to avoid the cops getting a lead on them didn't allow much time to beg properly. The tourists had been a little more giving at least, without having to be asked; they just saw children in need and handed out change.

The locals that passed by pretended not to see them; pretending to be in a hurry to get to or from work, and likely not wanting to end up in some kind of pick-pocketing scheme.

By the time lunchtime rolled around, they were both hungry and they shelled out the last of their cash to buy a meal from a street vendor. As he had promised himself, Jamie made sure that Sherry got the larger portion of the food.

"What do you think we should do next?" she asked, settling into a seat, eating slowly.

Jamie shrugged his shoulders. "Begging isn't going to get us much. I was thinking we could ask those nuns if they need someone to work with or for them, but I don't think they'll be able to understand me if I ask them. I mean, I don't see the harm in it."

He looked up, seeing one of the local gangs coming in closer. By now, they knew better than to get into any kind of dispute with those they came across. They were likely armed and connected with the local authorities, or at least, more connected than Jamie and Sherry were.

"I guess we could always try to work out a way to start pick-pocketing like the other kids," Jamie noted once they were safely away from the bullies. "Like you could make a scene for them, and I grab the money, and we run away."

"I don't... want to," Sherry said softly, shaking her head. "Don't want to steal."

"We may not have a choice. The bread place had less food than before, and there were more kids. Who knows how long those nuns are going to keep coming around, and in the meantime, we have no money and no way to get any? We need to find something."

Sherry nodded, sighing softly. "We'll figure something out. We have so far, right?"

She wasn't wrong, of course. They had been pushing their luck ever since they'd run away from the captors, and there was no telling how long that was going to last, but it wasn't as if there was an abundance of choices. They were going to need to rely on their wits a bit more over the next few days if they wanted to survive.

For the moment, though, it was another stay with the group of children outside. Jamie found that it was a little more difficult to sleep than it had been before.

Jasper Joshua West

Chapter Twenty-Three

NO MONEY, NO FOOD and no prospects. The bakery was closed for the day, by the looks of it, and there was no chance that they were going to find another place from which to get food. A couple of the local restaurants were open, but since it was Sunday, most of the people were at church. Even the owners of the restaurants, and the workers didn't want to give away free food without permission.

Jamie was starting to feel desperate. Sherry looked more tired than usual, and as the day started to get hotter, she was looking more and more sluggish as the seconds ticked by.

"I'm just hungry, that's all," she explained, shaking her head. Lunchtime came around, and still no food. He supposed that living on the street meant that they were going to have to get used to being hungry from time to time, but that realization wasn't going to make it any easier.

Around midday, when the sun was scorching, people began to leave church, going out for a meal at the local restaurants. Among the many people, most scowled and shouted in passing at the two in Spanish. Jamie couldn't understand what they were saying, but from the context, at least, it didn't sound good.

Suddenly, it looked like they were onto something. Sherry followed a restaurant worker out back behind a building, to find him discarding food. Some of it at least still smelled good, or maybe they were just too hungry to care. Still, Sherry pulled a bin over, to discover takeout boxes filled with rice, some even contained meat and vegetables.

"Better than nothing," Sherry said, choosing one that looked like it hadn't been touched. She ate it right there by the dumpster. Jamie was hungry too, and found himself taking a couple of bites, but once that edge of hunger was gone, the food started smelling a little off to him and he discarded what was left.

"Are you sure this food is okay?" Jamie asked. "It smells bad."

Sherry sniffed at her box. "Smells okay to me," she said.

He wasn't sure if he would be able to tell if the food was bad, though, and so as Sherry continued eating, he didn't stop her. They were no longer in a situation to be picky about what they ate.

Once they were finished, Sherry started to look better, acting a little more like herself as the day went on. They still didn't have much luck making money, and as they made their way back to the spot in which they had been spending the nights, Sherry was starting to look a little pale in the face.

"My stomach hurts," she complained, clutching at it. A second later she turned around and threw up on the sidewalk.

A couple of nearby strollers quickly backed away, cursing as they crossed the street. Jamie scowled at them, shaking his head as he helped Sherry straighten up.

"How do you feel?" he asked. She only managed to shake her head while clutching at her stomach.

They reached the spot again, but Sherry shivered and moaned softly, still looking like she was going to be sick. Jamie pressed his hand to her forehead but she didn't have a fever, which was odd. He remembered Sam shivering like this too when he was feeling sick, but he always had a fever when that happened.

One of the nuns approached them slowly, questioning them in Spanish. It was clear what she meant.

"Ella... enferma*," she's sick.* Jamie replied in halting Spanish. He made a gesture of eating, and then pointed at his stomach.

That was succinct enough, and the nun called one of the other nuns and told her about their situation.

"Vamos a la clínica*," go to the clinic* the other lady said helping Sherry on to her feet again.

"Where are we going?" Sherry asked, sounding sluggish.

"To get some help," Jamie replied, squeezing her hand again. "I hope."

Chapter Twenty-Four

THE ORPHANAGE WAS for girls only. Jamie wasn't sure how a rule like that was even instituted. He knew a thing or two about how religious orders worked, but if a boy got sick, would they just not help him?

It didn't really matter though. He wasn't sick, and Sherry was getting help. There wasn't much else that he could ask for except maybe a place to sit while he waited.

As it was, he was stuck outside, sitting on the sidewalk, waiting for news about Sherry. All he could be happy about was that they had at least gotten her some help.

The sound of the door opening behind him had Jamie jumping to his feet as a couple of young women walked out. They definitely didn't look like locals. One had blonde hair, while the other had brown curly hair, but they lacked the skin tone of the locals.

"Hey kid, is this your friend?" they asked, speaking very slowly, like he wasn't going to understand.

Was he starting to look like a local? He had been around long enough.

"They won't let me in to see her," Jamie said, trying to keep the tears from rolling down his cheeks.

"Yeah, they have some... rules in there," the blonde woman said. "Wait, your English is very good. You're not from around here, are you?"

Jamie looked around, feeling the twisted knot in his stomach return. "I... well, I'm from Massachusetts. My name is Jamie. My friend in there is Sherry, and she's from Canada. English Colombia or something."

"You mean British Colombia, right?" one of the women asked, and both exchanged a quick glance. "How did you end up here?"

Jamie clenched his teeth, feeling a couple of hot tears run down his cheeks despite his best effort. "I was..." his voice clamped up for a minute, not sure if they would believe the story, but he had to try. "We were kidnapped. It was a long time ago. We got away from the bad guys, but even the cops won't help us. Please, is Sherry okay?"

The two women exchanged another look, and the blonde woman stepped forward, lowering herself to eye level with him. Then she looked at her friend. "I remember all those kids getting kidnapped a while ago. Must have been over a year ago, actually. Do you think..."

"If he's telling the truth, that means that he and Sherry have been missing all that time."

If he was telling the truth? Jamie felt his cheeks flush. "I am telling the truth! Please, is Sherry going to be okay?"

"Hey, hey, now, it's okay, kiddo," the brunette said, putting her hand on his shoulder.

"I don't have money," Jamie said quickly. "But I have..." he pulled out his knife and the gun he'd fought off of the driver. "I got these off of the... well, the knife I got from the place where they were holding us. I stole the gun from the guy that drove Sherry away."

Both girls backed away at the sight of him bearing arms, and Jamie quickly realized his mistake, laying both on the ground. "Please, I don't have anything else to pay you with. Just make her feel better. There's no bullets in the gun."

They gingerly picked both up off the ground, trying to make out whether Jamie was actually trustworthy or not. He wondered if they dealt with this kind of thing often.

"Okay, I'm calling this in," the blonde nurse said, quickly turning to head back into the building.

She took both weapons with her. Jamie thought that meant that they were accepting his payment.

The brunette stayed with him. "Look... Jamie, right? We're going to be looking into getting you back with your parents, and Sherry too. In the meantime, we're going to be taking Sherry to a proper clinic to see a doctor, and you can come with us. Would you like that?"

Jamie could only manage a slow nod. He thought again about how Sam had said his parents weren't dead. Was he about to find out if it was true?

Chapter Twenty-Five

THIS WAS THE FIFTH SOLDIER to come into the room at the embassy and ask him the same series of questions. What was his name? What were his parents' names? How long had it been since he'd gotten to Colombia, and how had he arrived there? Where had he been kept this whole time? Jamie always gave them the same answers, which were correct, as far as he could recall. The submarine trip, staying with Carlos and Sam, the moving around, the house where the girls were taken out for rides.

He even told them about stabbing the man with the knife, but when he was asked if they were going to throw him in jail for it, they laughed, said no, and ended the interview.

He felt guilty for being annoyed with them. They had given him fresh clothes, and food as well as a bed to sleep in, which was also appreciated. They even let him see Sherry while she was recovering, letting them eat together and play old video games on the TV in her room.

This was as good as life had been for him since he had gotten here, but they were just asking him the same thing over and again and they never answered any of Jamie's questions.

He wondered if they couldn't just film him saying it all the one time, and that would be it. Jamie wasn't about to complain, though.

The men in fatigues finally told him and Sherry that their parents hadn't been killed by the mafia, in contrast to what they had been told, but were in fact on their way to fetch them. Jamie wasn't sure how to feel about that. Sherry was obviously very excited by the news, bouncing up and down in her hospital bed.

It was difficult. He had been gone for long enough for none of it to seem real. He knew he should be happy, but he was scared. It had been two years since he'd been kidnapped.

News that both their parents would be arriving in a few hours hit Jamie like a ton of bricks, and he didn't want to leave Sherry's side when they arrived. His parents looked exhausted. His dad had lost a great deal of weight, and his mother looked as if she hadn't slept in weeks. And they were all over him.

The touching, the hugging, the crying just felt odd somehow. Sherry and her parents looked so happy. Jamie wasn't sure what to make of that, but he forced a smile even though he could feel that his cheeks were wet from crying. They kept asking if he was okay, and Jamie didn't know what to say.

"We're going home, baby," Sharon said as she wrapped Jamie in her arms. "I've missed you so very, very much!"

Jamie could feel his chest convulsing as sobs pushed their way out. What was he going to do now? They wanted him to stay with them. And while he wanted that too, there was just something inside him saying that it wasn't right. Something was off about it but he couldn't tell what.

All he could do was clutch at his parents, hold them close, and hope they didn't notice.

Chapter Twenty-Six

JAMIE COULDN'T SLEEP. He had thought that was going to be a thing of the past. For all his exhaustion over the past two years, it was annoying to realize that now that it was all finished, he still couldn't sleep.

They were moved out of the embassy, and with Sherry on the mend, they were prepping both families to return to their respective homes; Jamie back to Boston, and Sherry back to Canada. Sherry's parents hadn't even let him say good-bye before whisking her away. Now they were all in a hotel near the airport, waiting for a flight that would take them all home and end this seemingly never-ending nightmare.

But there he was, just staring up at the ceiling. It wasn't that his mind was too busy to fall asleep, or like he had been trying to think up ways to avoid it.

But here, in bed, hearing his parents snoring quietly in their double bed and having one of his own just didn't feel right, somehow.

Jamie pushed himself up, carefully peeling the sheets off before walking over to the bathroom, silently closing the door and turning on the lights.

An odd sight, really. Jamie wasn't sure how someone could look in the mirror and feel alienated by the face looking back, but there was no denying that. He was thinner than before, but there was a lean musculature showing too. His cheeks were gaunt, and his eyes deep with a sort of redness and desperation. Having to fend for himself for two whole years was etched across his face as if one of his classmates had drawn it on with a magic marker.

Classmates. He was going home now, and probably going back to school, maybe play some kind of sport to pass the time, or maybe his parents would want him to play a musical instrument instead. Maybe sign up for some advanced placement classes.

He couldn't explain it, but after all this time away, the very concept just felt so foreign.

What were all of his friends going to think? Oh, wait, no, they would have all graduated, heading off to middle school or something. He would be stuck catching up with them because of his time spent here. Learning the kinds of skills that would help him survive here but would be useless back home.

Home?

It just didn't fit. He couldn't say why but thinking of his time back home just felt like someone else's memories and life that he was returning to.

Jamie looked back up into the mirror, and realized the stranger there was crying again, which he had been doing a lot of the past few days. He shook his head, moving away from the mirror and turned the bathroom light off. That was better.

He slipped out again, standing over his parents' bed. Practically strangers, really, and he knew that he was a stranger to them now too, despite all their talk of love and missing him. They even said that they had been looking for him all this time, which he believed.

It wasn't a conscious decision, but Jamie found himself picking up the bag that they'd packed for him and walking over to the door. He remembered the door number of Sherry's room too. He would see if she wanted to come with him.

He doubted she would because she was happy to be back with her family. She probably didn't see a stranger in the mirror like he did. She was a good girl and deserving of everything good in life.

"What the hell am I doing?" Jamie whispered to himself but couldn't stop putting one foot in front of the other until he was in front of her door, about to knock.

The lock clicked, and it opened. Sherry was standing in the frame, dressed in frilly pink pajamas.

"Hey," Jamie said softly.

"Hey back," she replied.

Chapter Twenty-Seven

SHARON GROANED SOFTLY, RISING FROM THE BED. She was used to being awake around this time; worrying about being in a foreign country ever since they'd arrived in Colombia, as well as worrying about her son. Jamie had made for a lot of sleepless nights, trying to find some new way to track her baby down whenever they lost his trail.

This was one of the first times that she could remember that she had managed to get some real sleep, but her body clock was still telling her that it was time to get up.

She grumbled and went to the bathroom, intending to go back to bed when she saw that Jamie's bed was empty.

The horror that filled her had her frozen for a few seconds, trying to convince herself that she was seeing things.

But no, the bed was empty. She ran over to Harry, shaking him awake.

"What… what?" he mumbled, still half-asleep, looking around and trying to put his glasses on.

"Jamie's gone," Sharon said loudly, shaking him again.

"He's been… wait, what?" Harry asked, waking up fully, and looking over to Jamie's bed. Sure enough, a second pair of eyes revealed what she already knew had happened. Harry climbed out of bed, and put on his clothes and they searched the room once more, just to make sure that Jamie wasn't just under a bed or on the balcony.

But he was gone.

Harry and Sharon left the room, and made their way to Sherry's parents' room. They were still asleep when Harry started pounding on their door, but sure enough, Sherry was gone as well.

"Do you think they went off together?" the father asked as they dressed and joined Sharon and Harry on their search.

"They've been together for months," Sharon pointed out. "I don't think that they would just leave each other alone after so long together. I think they would have gone together. The question is… where?"

They moved out to the lobby, where the night receptionists had not seen either of the children. The pair of parents were about to call the police for what felt like the millionth time when a bellboy on duty said that he'd seen two gringo children heading out to the playground outside the hotel.

Sharon, Harry and Sherry's parents quickly rushed out the back door into the dark playground, where they could see two dark figures. Sherry was on the swing, swaying gently and Jamie was sitting at the edge of the jungle gym.

They stopped talking immediately at the sight of the adults coming into the playground.

"Oh my God, Jamie!" Sharon shouted as she rushed over to wrap Jamie up in her arms. "Don't you know how worried we were? You can't just go wandering around again!"

Jamie said nothing in response. She supposed that he had been wandering around on his own, or with Sherry, for God knows how long, so there was no point in really telling him how unsafe it was to go out on his own.

He probably already knew the dangers better than she did.

Chapter Twenty-Eight

A GROUP OF PEOPLE was waiting for them at the airport when they arrived back. His family, sure, with both sets of grandparents, all his aunts and uncles, as well as a wide selection of others. Some were his friends, together with their families, as well as people that had heard about what had happened, and wanted to welcome him back. A couple of his old teachers had made up the welcome committee too.

There were even a couple of reporters with cameras, smiling and asking about how it felt to be back home. Jamie didn't know how to answer that. Would they understand if he explained that all he felt was confused?

Probably not.

His parents were quick to intervene, saying that he was still recovering and was in no shape to answer any questions, quickly moving him to the waiting car. Nobody really wanted to know about what happened to the other children who had been kidnapped. Some had been recovered, sure, but a lot of them were still missing.

Nobody remembered them. Maybe they'd forgotten about Jamie too, and were only reminded when he was finally brought back.

It didn't really matter. Jamie was quickly pushed into a car, where his grandparents were hugging him and asking how he felt. A small party had been arranged once they got back to the house, that Jamie had almost forgotten about.

His mother's parents were talking about how they knew a doctor that was good with children who could examine him. One of his aunts talked about how she knew a child therapist that Jamie could talk to, but all Harry and Sharon could say was that they were just happy to have their baby boy back.

It was weird, though; he didn't feel back. People were talking to him, but also practically ignored him. They were talking about him, but never once wanted to dig deeper into what had happened to him, or the other children. It was like they didn't even want to know.

Everyone was talking about how it was just the happy ending that they had been hoping and praying for. If that was the case, why didn't Jamie feel like it was happy, or the end?

They didn't get him back to school immediately, of course. An extensive medical checkup had a doctor telling his parents that he was marginally malnourished and showing signs of injuries which hadn't healed properly, as well as scars that Jamie had almost forgotten about.

Otherwise, he was as physically healthy as any other boy his age. The psychologist said that mentally was another matter, but Jamie could hear the man tell his parents that he was clammed up, refusing to talk about what had happened while he was missing.

Of course, he wasn't going to talk to them. They didn't even want to know about it, right? About how he missed Sam and Sherry. People didn't want to know that. All they wanted was for him to put on a smile and say that he was getting better. That was the happy ending that they wanted to hear.

He pulled out his phone and dialed the number that his parents had given him. Sherry didn't have a phone of her own, but her house did.

"Hello?" answered a woman's voice.

"Hi," Jamie said softly, clearing his throat and then speaking again. "This is Jamie. Can I talk with Sherry, please?"

There was a pause as Jamie sensed that the woman – Sherry's mother – didn't want to think about the situation anymore either, and that Jamie calling to talk with her daughter wasn't helping.

"Sure," the woman said with a soft, fake chuckle. "I'll get her, just a moment."

A few seconds passed, and Jamie could hear the woman's muffled voice, asking if Sherry wanted to talk to Jamie.

Another pause.

"Jamie?"

It was Sherry's voice. She sounded healthy at least, like she was getting better after her sickness.

"Hey... hey, Sherry," Jamie said, feeling his voice crack. "Are you okay? How's it going in Canada?"

"I don't know," she replied, honestly.

"Yeah. I feel the same way."

They didn't speak for a few seconds. It was nice to just know that she was there, even if all he could hear was her breathing. He missed her, he realized. Weird.

"How about you? You sound tired."

Jamie blinked. "I... I haven't been sleeping."

"Why not?"

"Because..."

He didn't know what to say. Nightmares were something that he'd been dealing with since the kidnapping, but they hadn't stopped him from sleeping before.

"I just don't feel right," he said, finally.

"I know the feeling." Sherry agreed. "I keep thinking about the other children that we left behind. My mom says that a few of the kidnapped kids were recovered, but a lot weren't. I thought after we got back and told the cops what we knew, they would find the other children, but I feel like they've given up. How can they just give up?"

Her voice was cracking and she was tearing up, and all Jamie wanted to do was reach out and grab her hand, and squeeze it like he had so many times while they were together on the streets.

"I miss you," she whispered softly.

"Yeah… I miss you, too," Jamie said, trying not to cry. He was failing, and a couple of hot tears ran down his cheek.

He brushed them away quickly. "Look, I've got to go, it's late. I'll talk to you soon, okay?"

"Okay, call me tomorrow," she said. She sounded so sad that Jamie longed to be there to comfort her.

The line cut off, and Jamie put the cordless phone down on his desk. He then sat for a long moment staring at it, deep in thought. Finally, his mom tapped softly on his bedroom door and told him it was time for bed. Jamie opened the door, handed her the telephone, and went to brush his teeth.

Epilogue

JAMIE RETURNED TO SCHOOL, and it was good to be back home where he no longer feared for his safety on a daily basis. The stories about his captivity, escape and having to fend for himself, together with the scars to prove it all, made him popular amongst his peers, but he didn't feel like he belonged anymore. His classmates still acted like little children, while Jamie, who had spent over a year away, felt more like an adult now. He didn't care about any of the stupid concerns of other 12-year-olds and he couldn't talk to them about what was really on his mind.

Jamie couldn't talk to his parents either; he had tried, and they were willing to listen, but they didn't know what to say. His mother had mentioned that a counselor might be able to help, but Jamie didn't think so. The only person he could talk to who really understood, was Sherry. They sometimes talked about what they had been through together and what would have happened had they not escaped. But they mostly spoke about what the other kidnapped children were still going through and what people could do about it.

Harry and Sharon were supportive of this, but they thought he was too young for a cell phone. They did give Jamie a phone card so that he could call Sherry any time without too much expense. They even promised to take Jamie to Vancouver to visit Sherry in the summer.

When Jamie wasn't busy talking to Sherry or doing his homework, he spent most of his time reading about kidnapping and human trafficking. He was appalled to learn that thousands of children, mostly girls, were victims of human trafficking in the United States every year. When he looked at worldwide statistics, the number climbed into the millions. He and Sherry often spoke about this and while she didn't share his obsession for research, she agreed that something needed to be done, and they vowed that one day they would make a difference.

Second Hand

Dear Reader,

I hope you enjoyed the story. **I've included a FREE BOOK below and a sample of another book on the next page**.

It would be awesome if you could let others know what you thought of my book by leaving a review on Amazon!

Thanks for reading,

JJW jjwestauthor@gmail.com

Get your FREE copy of Escaped!

bookHip.com/lkcwpk

Just type in bookHip.com/lkcwpk

Keep reading for a free sample of: GROUNDED

Second Hand

See GROUNDED in store (Amazon USA)

Chapter 1

Day 1: Sunday

DENNIS COLEMAN WOKE up first. Light was already streaming in around the curtains. He looked at Sarah, who was sleeping peacefully on her side of the bed, her light brown hair covering her face. He watched her sleeping for a moment, then he turned and picked up his smartphone from the bedside table and checked the time. 7:56. Normally the kids were up at sunrise and they woke him and Sarah up not long after, so there was no need for an alarm clock on the weekends. To add to his good mood, there were no new emails waiting for him this morning, probably for the first time in months. It looked like it was going to be a good Sunday.

Dennis used the bathroom, stood in the hallway listening to the quiet for a moment, then headed back into the bedroom. He was still a little sleepy, and he was also hoping that he and Sarah could make love before heading downstairs. He nuzzled up against her and planted a kiss on her cheek. She moaned but did not stir.

He closed his eyes but instead of drifting off, his mind wandered to his messages. He had certainly sent out enough yesterday, and because of the time difference, his clients in Asia usually replied while he was sleeping. Perhaps they had all decided to take Sunday off for once and he would hear from them in the evening.

As if in answer to his thoughts, his phone chimed with an incoming message. He snatched it up to find it wasn't an email but a text message. The number was blocked and the message read: "YOU ARE ALL GROUNDED!" Dennis instantly dismissed it as some sort of spam, and he was about to put the phone back on the table when he noticed there was no cell signal. He must have just lost the signal as it had to have been working for the text to come in.

The Wi-Fi icon was also missing from the status bar on his phone, which was strange because he always kept his phone connected, even while he was sleeping. Opening the menu, he determined that the phone's wireless adaptor was turned on but couldn't detect any wireless networks in range. Dennis scowled as he considered the money he had spent setting up three Wi-Fi access points in the house. Even if the one on the second floor wasn't working, he should still be able to get a weak signal from the one downstairs.

Normally the internet going down in the house wouldn't have been a big deal, but with no cell signal, his mobile data wouldn't be working either, which meant his clients had no way of getting in touch with him. He was a very successful man, a leader in his field, but that could change really fast if he was unavailable when his clients needed him. There was, after all, plenty of competition in the business.

Dennis sighed again, put on a bathrobe, and went to have a look at the Wi-Fi router which was mounted on the ceiling in the hallway. The power light was glowing steadily, but all of the other lights were dark. He wasn't exactly sure what all of those little lights were supposed to indicate, but the fact that they were all off was not a good sign, he was sure. He had glanced at the router before and normally there were several lights glowing, some of them steadily and some of them flashing randomly. He assumed there must either be something wrong with the router or there was no internet signal coming in. Dennis didn't know what to do besides turning it off and turning it back on again.

On the other side of the router, he found a couple of wires going in and a button that said PWR under it. He pressed the button once to turn it off, then again to turn it back on. Then he looked at the lights on the front of the unit again. All of the lights came on momentarily, then they all went off except for the one that had been on before and the DSL light which began flashing on and off at even intervals. Dennis checked his phone again and found that he still had no Wi-Fi signal. He decided to go check downstairs where there was an identical router mounted high on the wall behind the sofa.

Dennis stood on the couch to get a closer look at the lights and found only the power light was on. He reached for the power button hidden on top of the unit and pushed it, causing the power light to go off. He then pushed it again, causing all of the lights to glow momentarily before they all went out except for the PWR light. As had been the case upstairs, the DSL light began flashing slowly on and off. He checked his phone again to find that there was still no cell signal or Wi-Fi network available.

Dennis decided it was unlikely that both routers had stopped working overnight and that the problem must be the internet line coming into the house. He found the phone number for the internet company on his phone and hit send before remembering that his cell signal was also down.

Annoyed, Dennis headed back upstairs to his office where there was a landline. He'd insisted on getting one when they first moved in. Though he had only used it a few times in the four years they'd been living in the house, every now and then a situation arose where something other than a cell phone was required. As he reached the top of the stairs and headed for his office, a feeling of dread struck him. He stopped and opened the text message again, reading the cryptic missive:

YOU ARE ALL GROUNDED!

See GROUNDED in store (Amazon USA)

More by JJ West

USA: bit.ly/JasperWestBooks

INTERNATIONAL: bit.ly/JasperWestWorld

Printed in Great Britain
by Amazon